The Pied Piper
and the
Wrong Song

by Laura North and Scoular Anderson

W
FRANKLIN WATTS
LONDON•SYDNEY

This story is based on the traditional fairy tale,
The Pied Piper of Hamelin but with a new twist.
You can read the original story in
Hopscotch Fairy Tales. Can you make
up your own twist for the story?

First published in 2013 by
Franklin Watts
338 Euston Road
London
NW1 3BH

Franklin Watts Australia
Level 17/207 Kent Street
Sydney
NSW 2000

Text © Laura North 2013
Illustrations © Scoular Anderson 2013

The rights of Laura North to be identified as the author
and Scoular Anderson as the illustrator of this Work have been asserted
in accordance with the Copyright, Designs and Patents Act, 1988.

A CIP catalogue record for this book is available
from the British Library.

ISBN 978 1 4451 1632 7 (hbk)

ISBN 978 1 4451 1638 9 (pbk)

Series Editor: Melanie Palmer
Series Advisor: Catherine Glavina
Series Designer: Peter Scoulding

Printed in China

Franklin Watts is a division of
Hachette Children's Books,
an Hachette UK company
www.hachette.co.uk

To Dylan — L.N.

In the town of Hamelin

there were rats everywhere.

"The Pied Piper can help us,"
said the Mayor.
"He plays a magic pipe that
makes the rats go away."

4

So the Pied Piper arrived in town.
"I will get rid of your rats!"
he promised.

Rid-a-Rat

"If you can do that," said the Mayor, "I will give you ten bags of gold."

"No problem," said the Pied Piper.
He took out his magic pipe and
started to play.

The rats looked up at the Pied
Piper. Not one of them moved.

But one by one, all the cows in the town started to follow the Pied Piper's magic song.

"Oh no!" said the Mayor.

"What are you doing?"

"I don't know what went wrong!"
said the Pied Piper. "Let me
try again."

This time all the pigs began to
follow the Pied Piper, and
danced in a line to his tune.

"Come back!" the Mayor shouted after the pigs. "There goes all our bacon!"

"Oh dear," said the Pied Piper.

"This doesn't usually happen."

15

"Let me try again," said the Pied Piper. He started to play.

17

All the farmers started to dance
along merrily, heading for the hills.

The farmers left their gates open and their farm animals escaped!

The goats were eating the flowers.

The pigs were sitting in armchairs.

And the cows got into bed.

One clever boy called Peter had an idea. "Take these," he said, and gave everyone earmuffs.

"You won't be able to hear anything that the Pied Piper plays."

The Pied Piper said,

"I know I've got it right this time!"

He played his magic pipe. But

nobody moved at all.

25

No one heard a thing.

Not one rat, cow, pig or farmer.

27

And the rats were still everywhere!
The Mayor gave up. The townspeople
paid the Pied Piper to go away
instead!

29

Put these pictures in the correct order.
Which event do you think is most important?
Now try writing the story in your own words!